The Meanest Thing to Say

The Meanest Thing to Say

by Bill Cosby

Illustrated by Varnette P. Honeywood

SCHOLASTIC INC.
New York   Toronto   London   Auckland   Sydney

Library of Congress Cataloging-in-Publication Data

Cosby, Bill, 1937-
    The meanest thing to say / Bill Cosby ; illustrated by Varnette P. Honeywood.
        p.   cm.— (A little Bill book)
    "Cartwheel books."
    Summary: When a new boy in his second grade class tries to get the other students to play a game that involves saying the meanest thing possible to one another, Little Bill shows him a better way to make friends.
    ISBN 0-590-95616-7
    [1. Behavior— Fiction. 2. Schools— Fiction.]   I. Honeywood, Varnette P., ill.   II. Title.
III. Series. IV. Series: Cosby, Bill, 1937- Little Bill book.
PZ7.C8185Me   1997
[E] — dc20   96-32791
                                                                                                                  CIP
                                                                                                                   AC

10 9 8 7 6 5 4 3 2

Printed in the U.S.A.   23
First printing, September 1997

To Ennis,
"Hello, friend,"
B.C.

To the Cosby Family,
Ennis's perseverance against the odds
is an inspiration to us all,
V.P.H

Dear Parent:

Sooner or later, most children — on the street, the playground, or at school — meet other children who are deliberately mean. When this happens, there are several options for a child who is being picked on. Too often, the picked-on child's immediate response is either to fight back or to attempt a protective retreat. Retreating is preferable since fighting back will certainly escalate the conflict and may result in injury to both children. Not the best solution!

This story presents a sensible alternative course of action. With guidance from his parents, Little Bill learns to cope with a hostile child by controlling his own reactions. At school, he manipulates the confrontation without stooping to being "mean" himself. Heeding his father's advice, he gains the upper hand by saying "So?" to the angry boy's taunts. When Little Bill simply refuses to participate, the nasty name-calling falls flat. His strategy succeeds! Finding that his tactics aren't working, the deflated "mean" kid retreats in embarrassment.

But the story doesn't end there. The "mean" youngster is feeling insecure and lonely himself! — perhaps because he is the new boy in his class. As Little Bill reaches out, inviting him to play and be a friend, we learn that even a potential bully, when approached with kindness yet firmness, may yield.

These tactics may not always be practical, but this book shows your child that there are ways to resolve conflicts with other children without losing face or resorting to violence. In the process, a misbehaving kid may have a chance to change and be welcomed as a friend.

Alvin F. Poussaint, MD
Clinical Professor of Psychiatry
Harvard Medical School and
Judge Baker Children's Center
Boston, MA

Chapter One

Hello, friend. My name is Little Bill. My teacher is Miss Murray.

One day, a new boy, Michael Reilly, came into our class. It didn't take long for him to start trouble — just until recess.

I walked to the basketball court with my friends—Andrew, José, and Kiku. My cousin, Fuchsia, was waiting for us. She's in a different class.

José was dribbling when Michael showed up.

"I know a better game," Michael said. "It's called Playing the Dozens. You get twelve chances to say something mean to a person. The meanest thing wins."

"I'll start," José said. "Andrew is a lousy basketball player."

"José hops with the frogs in the sixth grade lab," said Andrew.

"But Andrew eats frogs for dinner," José said.

Kiku looked sick.

"You shoot like a girl,"
Michael said to me.

"*I* shoot like a girl," said Fuchsia. She
took the ball, walked back a few steps, and
aimed. *Swish.* A perfect shot.
  "Yes, baby!" she said.

Michael pointed his finger at me.
"I'm not finished with you," he said.
Just then, the bell rang.
"Tomorrow!" Michael said.

Chapter Two

I couldn't do my homework. I was thinking about what to say to Michael tomorrow. There had to be a million mean things to say to him. But I was so mad that I couldn't think of any.

I stood on my bed and flexed my muscles. I started jumping and yelling. "Watch out, Reilly-man. I am the best—the greatest—the smartest kid in the world!"

Soon my mother was at the door. "Young man, stop jumping on that bed. NOW!" said Mom. I jumped down with a loud crash.

I went to the dinner table. Macaroni and cheese. Fantastic! My great-grandmother — everyone calls her Alice the Great — was already at the table.

"Little Bill, what was all that noise about?" she asked.

"I'm getting ready for a contest tomorrow," I said.

"A boxing match?" asked Mom.

"It's called Playing the Dozens, because you have twelve chances to say something mean to the other guy. I'm going to make a list of a million mean things to say. If I study that list really hard, I can't lose."

That's when my dad walked into the kitchen. He's Big Bill.

"Hey, buddy, what's this I hear about studying? Big test tomorrow?" he asked.

"No, dear. Our son is in a contest," Mom said. "He has to come up with a million mean things to say to someone at school."

"When I was a boy, we called that 'ranking,'" Dad said.

"This new kid said that I shoot like a girl!"

Dad shrugged his shoulders and said, "So?"

"D-a-d. Michael Reilly is a creep!"

"So?"

"Dad! He's bad."

My dad was about to say it again . . .

"Soooooo?"

"Is that all you can say?" I asked. "So. So. So. You've said it about a million times. I . . . I . . ."

When I looked around the table, everyone was smiling.

"It's easier than studying a million mean things," Dad said.

He got up and jumped around the kitchen like a boxer. He raised his hands in the air and said, "I was the World 'Ranking' Champion!"

And the rest of us said, "So!?"

Chapter Three

The next day, Michael was waiting for me in the school yard. And I was ready for him!

"You smell like old egg salad," Michael started.

"So?" I said.

"So you're a stupid nerd who looks like a slimy slug," Michael said.

"So?"

"You're a teacher's pet with bugs living in your hair," said Michael.

I thought that was funny, and I laughed and said, "So?"

Soon, the other kids were laughing. Michael was getting angry.

"This isn't how you play the game! You have to call me names. Call me stupid! Call me mean! I'm ugly!" Michael yelled.

I laughed harder. He was funny. "So?"

Michael yelled even more. "You're supposed to be getting angry. You should be crying by now. What's wrong with you anyway?"

"You're funny," I said.

The bell rang.

"I'm going inside," Michael said as he ran off.

I looked at Andrew. "So?" we said at the same time. And we laughed.

Then we walked to our classroom. Michael was sitting all alone at his desk. I kind of liked him and I felt sorry for him.

"We're playing basketball during recess. Do you want to play?" I asked.

"Sure," Michael said quietly.

"You can be on my team," Andrew said.

"He's a lousy player," I said, grinning at Andrew.

Michael smiled, too, and said, "So?"

We all laughed together.

Outside, I held out my hand
and Michael gave me a high five.

Bill Cosby is one of America's best-loved storytellers, known for his work as a comedian, actor, and producer. His books for adults include *Fatherhood, Time Flies, Love and Marriage* and *Childhood.* Mr. Cosby holds a doctoral degree in education from the University of Massachusetts.

HOWARD L. BINGHAM

Varnette P. Honeywood, a graduate of Spelman College and the University of Southern California, is a Los Angeles-based impressive genre painter. Her work is included in many collections throughout the United States, Japan and Africa and has appeared on adult trade book jackets and in a children's book, *Shake It to the One That You Love the Best.*

Books in the LITTLE BILL series:

The Meanest Thing to Say
All the kids are playing a new game.
You have to be mean to win it.
Can Little Bill be a winner...
and be nice, too?

The Best Way to Play
Little Bill and his friends want the
new Space Rangers video game.
But their parents won't buy it.
How can Little Bill and his
friends have fun without it?

The Treasure Hunt
Little Bill searches his room
for his best treasure.
What he finds is a great big surprise!